For my drawing teachers:
Charlie Lume, Amy Fichter, David Zosel,
the late Karen Johnson,
and my dad.

ON A BRIGHT AUGUST MORNING,
Miss Maple flies home. She has hurried ahead
of the flock to get ready for her guests.

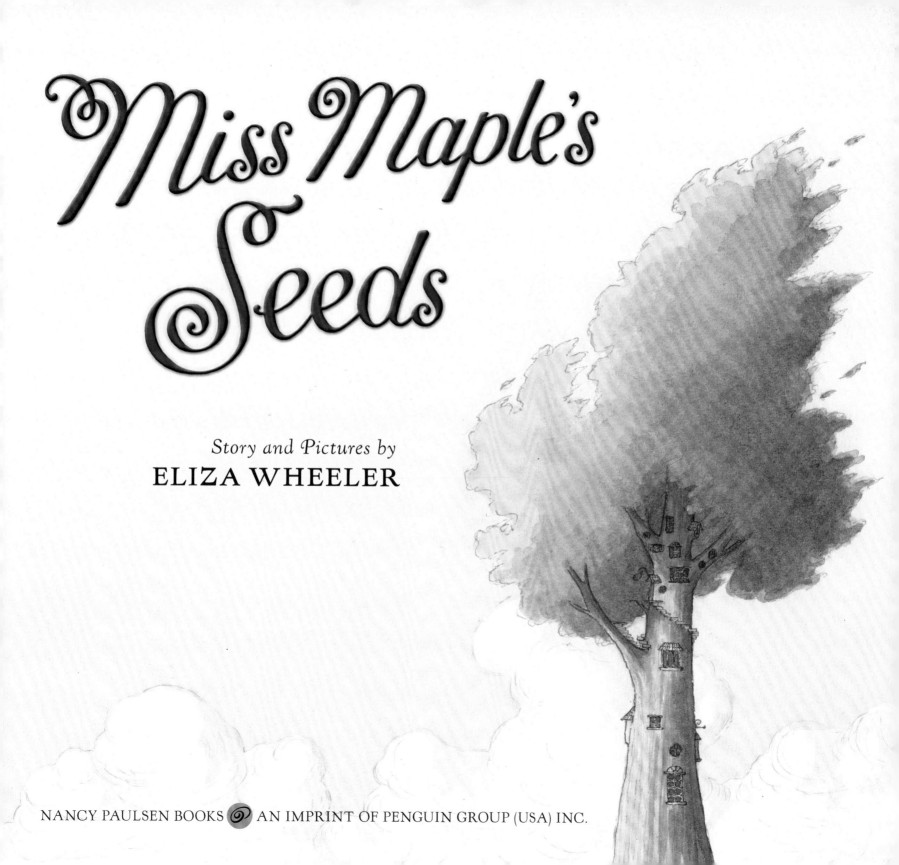

Miss Maple's Seeds

Story and Pictures by
ELIZA WHEELER

NANCY PAULSEN BOOKS ✺ AN IMPRINT OF PENGUIN GROUP (USA) INC.

NANCY PAULSEN BOOKS
A division of Penguin Young Readers Group.
Published by The Penguin Group.
Penguin Group (USA) Inc., 375 Hudson Street, New York, NY 10014, U.S.A.
Penguin Group (Canada), 90 Eglinton Avenue East, Suite 700, Toronto, Ontario M4P 2Y3, Canada
(a division of Pearson Penguin Canada Inc.).
Penguin Books Ltd, 80 Strand, London WC2R 0RL, England.
Penguin Ireland, 25 St. Stephen's Green, Dublin 2, Ireland (a division of Penguin Books Ltd).
Penguin Group (Australia), 250 Camberwell Road, Camberwell, Victoria 3124, Australia (a division of Pearson Australia Group Pty Ltd).
Penguin Books India Pvt Ltd, 11 Community Centre, Panchsheel Park, New Delhi - 110 017, India.
Penguin Group (NZ), 67 Apollo Drive, Rosedale, Auckland 0632, New Zealand (a division of Pearson New Zealand Ltd).
Penguin Books South Africa, Rosebank Office Park, 181 Jan Smuts Avenue, Parktown North 2193, South Africa.
Penguin China, B7 Jiaming Center, 27 East Third Ring Road North, Chaoyang District, Beijing 100020, China.
Penguin Books Ltd, Registered Offices: 80 Strand, London WC2R 0RL, England.

Design by Ryan Thomann. Title lettering by Ian Schoenherr. Text set in Kennerley.
The art was created with dip pens, India ink, and watercolors on Arches 140 lb cold-pressed paper.

Library of Congress Cataloging-in-Publication Data
Wheeler, Eliza. Miss Maple's seeds / Eliza Wheeler. p. cm. Summary: After gathering lost seeds during the summer,
a kind woman tends and instructs them throughout the fall and winter before sending them out in the spring to find roots of their own.
[1. Seeds—Fiction.] I. Title. PZ7.W5623Mis 2013 [E]—dc23 2012023867
ISBN 978-0-399-25792-6
Special markets ISBN 978-0-399-25593-9 Not for Resale
3 5 7 9 10 8 6 4 2

Miss Maple has traveled all summer long, searching the land for orphan seeds that got lost during the spring planting. She hopes to help them grow strong here in her tall maple tree, and get ready for next year's planting.

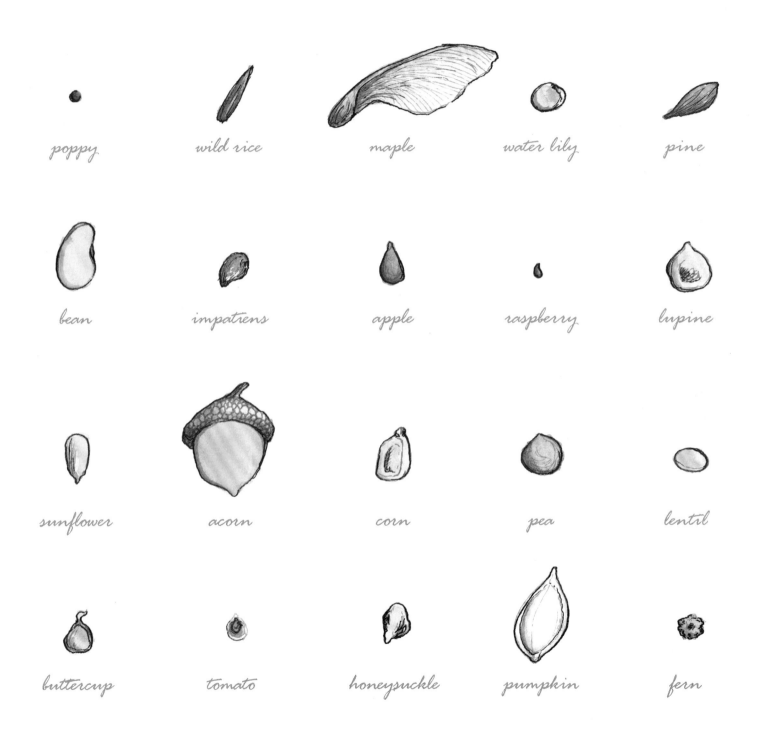

poppy

wild rice

maple

water lily

pine

bean

impatiens

apple

raspberry

lupine

sunflower

acorn

corn

pea

lentil

buttercup

tomato

honeysuckle

pumpkin

fern

She learns each seed by heart, all similar yet none the same. "Take care, my little ones," Miss Maple says, "for the world is big and you are small."

Miss Maple takes them on field trips to learn about being a seed.
Some will be carried by the river and land in soft, muddy soils.
Friends of the river will help them bloom in safe places.

They tour the grassy fields and thick forests. Many seeds will be blown here, where rich soil will keep their pods healthy, and the sun and rain will help them grow tall. In bustling gardens, seeds must take care to stay clear of weedy characters.

Snuggled in each night, Miss Maple reads
flower tales by firefly light. Before going to bed,
she whispers, "Take care, my little ones, for the
world is big and you are small."

Winter comes with the snow, a time to stay cozy and dry. Neighborhood friends gather to share their supplies of hot maple syrup, old corn husks, and juicy fruit rinds. Together they pass the long months with stories and songs.

When spring comes, thunderstorms pour curtains of rain. "Don't be afraid—raindrops help us grow," Miss Maple says to the seeds. They learn to dance and burrow down into the muddy ground.

On a windy May morning, the last spring petals drift
down from the sky. The time has come for Miss Maple
to send her seeds off to find roots of their own.

They set out on an exciting new journey into the wide unknown. Some seeds will take root in nearby gardens, while others will travel on distant winds and faraway tides.

As Miss Maple gazes out across the land below,
she whispers, "Take care, my little ones, for the
world is big and you are small. But never forget . . .

". . . even the grandest of trees once had to grow up from the smallest of seeds."

Into the evening, she sips her green tea in the quiet hollow of the old maple tree.

But the end of each season is a start to the next. One summer morning, Miss Maple grabs her willowweed hat, whistles a merry tune, and sets off to follow the faraway call of other lost seeds, waiting to be found.

Miss Maple has given them guidance and love, and now her part in their story has come to an end. They say their good-byes with sweet memories past and bright futures ahead.